WILD ANIMALS OF AMERICA ABC

PHOTOGRAPHS AND TEXT BY

· HOPE RYDEN ·

LODESTAR BOOKS   DUTTON   NEW YORK

ACKNOWLEDGEMENTS

For assistance in shooting pictures of several animals in this book,
I wish to thank personnel at the Bronx Zoo; the New York Aquarium;
the Jamaica Bay National Wildlife Refuge on Long Island; Lifeline
for Wildlife Rehabilitation Center in Stony Point, New York; the Turtle
Back Zoo in West Orange, New Jersey; the Arizona-Sonora Desert
Museum in Tucson; Denali National Park in Alaska; and Lake Ridge
Golf Course in Reno, Nevada.

Copyright © 1988 by Hope Ryden

Library of Congress Cataloging-in-Publication Data
Ryden, Hope.
  Wild animals of America ABC.
  Summary: Presents photographs and gives end notes about
characteristics of wild animals found in different parts of
North America, arranged alphabetically from alligator to
zone-tailed hawk.
  1. Zoology—North America—Pictorial works—Juvenile literature.
2. Animals—Pictorial works—Juvenile literature. [1.Zoology.
2. Animals—Habits and behavior. 3. Alphabet] I. Title.
QL155.R93 1988 599 87-31127
ISBN 0-525-67245-1

Published in the United States by Lodestar Books,
an affiliate of Dutton Children's Books,
a division of Penguin Books USA Inc.

Editor: Virginia Buckley   Designer: Riki Levinson

Printed in Hong Kong by South China Printing Co.
First Edition   W   10 9 8 7 6 5 4 3 2

About this book

Many American children know more about wild animals in faraway countries—say, lions and tigers and elephants—than about the beautiful wild creatures that live in the United States. For this reason, I have created an alphabet book of American animals.

Of course, I could not include all the wonderful wild creatures that live here. The book would be too long. I did make sure that animals from many different parts of the country appeared in it. So if you happen to live in Alaska, you can enjoy looking at a picture of Alaska's beautiful lynx or grizzly bear. But you might not be acquainted with some other creatures in this book. For example, you might never have seen a kit fox, a tiny desert animal that lives in Arizona, New Mexico, Nevada, and California. Or perhaps you are a reader who comes from Florida or Louisiana. Then you will surely recognize the first animal pictured in this book, the alligator, which lives in your swamps.

Some of the creatures on the following pages live in water, others are able to fly, and still others walk or crawl on the ground. If you want to learn how these animals live, turn to the back of the book and read about them.

I hope this book will start you looking for the wild animals that live near you. America is home to many fascinating creatures. You could have a lot of fun getting to know them.

Alligator

Beaver

B

Coyote

Deer

Elk

E

Flying squirrel

F

Grizzly bear

G

Harbor seal

Iguana

Jackrabbit

J

Kit fox

Lynx

L

Mountain lion

M

Newt

Otter

Possum

Quail

Raccoon

Skunk

S

Turtle

T

Urchin

Vole

Wolf

Xanthid crab

Yellow-bellied marmot

Zone-tailed hawk

Z

About these animals

Alligators are fast swimmers and live in swamps. Females guard the eggs they lay in their big grass nests. They also protect the babies that hatch. Baby alligators are tiny, but grown alligators are huge, sometimes more than twelve feet long. Even so, they are often hard to see. When an alligator suns itself, it looks like a log.

Beavers spend most of their time in the ponds they make by damming streams. They also build big stick lodges in which the whole family sleeps during the day. At night they climb up on land to cut the trees they need for food and lumber. Many kinds of animals live in the ponds that beavers make. Baby beavers are called kits.

Coyotes are much like dogs. They wag their tails and bark and lick one another's faces. They live together in packs. Every member of a pack helps care for the pups that are born to one female. They all bring mice and rabbits for the young to eat. Coyotes often get together to howl. It is their way of singing.

Deer are fast and graceful runners. A newborn deer, called a fawn, hides in brush while its mother goes off to feed on leaves and berries. It lies perfectly still so it will not be found by animals that eat deer. Every few hours its mother returns so it can nurse. When it grows older and stronger, it follows her about.

Elk are a lot like deer, only bigger. Male elk grow large antlers, called racks, on top of their heads. These heavy antlers fall off in winter, but new ones start to grow in right away. By fall the males' new antlers are bigger and have more branches than the ones they lost. They use these pointed weapons to fight each other for females.

Flying squirrels glide through the air even though they don't have real wings. A fold of skin between their hind and front legs acts as a kind of sail to keep them aloft. Flying squirrels live in hollow trees and come out only at night. Their big eyes help them see in the dark.

Grizzly bears sleep in caves all winter long. That is when a mother bear gives birth to cubs, usually twins. In spring when the family wakes up, they are very hungry and will eat anything they can find, including roots, grasses, grubs, and other animals. In Alaska, bears like to fish for salmon. Grizzlies can be blond, brown, or black.

Harbor seals spend most of their time in water, even though they must breathe air. A seal pup can swim, but it stays on a beach until it is strong. If a high wave washes it into the sea, it closes its nostrils to keep water out. Grown seals can stay underwater twenty minutes without breathing. This gives them time to catch the fish they eat.

Iguanas, like all lizards, are cold-blooded and must warm themselves in the sun before they can get going in the morning. This desert iguana is the fastest lizard in the world. When chased, it stands up and runs on its hind legs. Although it may look dangerous, the desert iguana is harmless. It likes to eat creosote flowers.

Jackrabbits move about by hopping, but when chased by an enemy, they run flat out like a racehorse. Many animals eat the jackrabbit, so it is always alert. To avoid being noticed, it crouches low and holds absolutely still. When closely pursued, it runs in zigzags. Jackrabbit babies are born with their eyes open, ready to run.

Kit foxes live in the hot deserts of the West and wait until night to come out of their cool underground burrows. Their big ears help them to hear and catch animals in the dark. When a female kit fox is caring for cubs, her mate brings her food to eat. He catches mice and rats by pouncing on them with his front feet.

Lynx are a lot like house cats with bobbed tails. They clean their fur with their tongues, and chase and play with anything that moves. Their oversized paws allow them to walk on snow without sinking in. This makes it possible for them to catch their favorite food, the snowshoe hare. Lynx are colored so they are hard to see in summer.

Mountain lions once lived in wild places all across America. Today they are rare. Because this cat is so big, it must hunt and eat large animals, like deer. To catch one, it moves slowly and silently, then makes its pounce in a sudden rush. Mountain lions can scream like tomcats. When happy, they purr like kittens.

Newts begin life as tiny larvae in water. When one inch long, they turn bright red and climb up on land. There they live for several years, eating insects and hiding under leaves. When it is time to breed, they change their costume again and go back to living in water. Unlike lizards, newts do not have scales.

Otters are the most playful of wild animals. They love water games and dive over and under each other just for fun. Sometimes one will float on its back while holding a stone or even a live turtle in its paws. In winter otters like to coast downhill, using their bellies as sleds. Otters often live in ponds that beavers make.

Possums play dead when attacked by hungry foxes or bobcats. Sometimes this trick saves their lives. When children pretend to be asleep, they are said to be "playing possum." Possum babies are carried in a special pouch on their mother's belly until they are old enough to ride on her back. Another name for possum is opossum.

Quails come out of hiding early in the morning and late in the afternoon, and scurry about the ground like chickens. "Bob-white! Bob-white!" they call to one another. A quail chick isn't kept in a nest and fed by its mother like a baby robin or bluebird. It can walk about and peck for seeds and bugs as soon as it hatches.

Raccoons poke their front paws into everything. They turn over rocks, looking for insects; they grope in water for crayfish; they stick their five-fingered, handlike paws into nests, feeling for eggs; they can even open garbage cans and unlatch shed doors. Maybe that is why some people call them "masked bandits."

Skunks eat just about anything they come across, including birds' eggs, fruit, and even honeybees. A skunk seems quite defenseless, but it has a secret weapon that keeps enemies away. It sprays them with a terrible smelling oil that lasts for days. When a skunk raises its bushy tail, it is time to get out of the way!

Turtles, when frightened, draw their heads and legs into their hard shells. This snapping turtle lives in water, but she climbed onto land to lay her eggs. Sometimes she floats just below the water's surface, waiting for a duckling or frog to swim by. If she can grab the unsuspecting creature, she will pull it underwater.

Urchins are covered with sharp spines and live in the ocean. They use their spines as legs to propel themselves about. Urchins must swallow a lot of sand to get what tiny bits of food have sunk to the ocean bottom. Later they cast up the sand. Many kinds of urchins live in the sea. Some are bright purple.

Voles spend a lot of time underground and are hard to see. When they do tunnel up to feed on grass and seeds, they travel along special paths which they make in the grass and beneath the snow. Because voles are eaten by many animals, they try hard to keep out of sight. A vole looks like a fat mouse with a short tail.

Wolves are a lot like coyotes, only bigger. For this reason they need to eat more. That is why they must hunt large animals, such as moose and caribou and deer. This is dangerous work, and so wolves hunt together in packs. Before setting out, all the wolves get together and howl. Perhaps they are giving one another a pep talk.

Xanthid crabs live in the ocean but cannot swim. Unlike other ocean crabs, they have no paddles on their last pair of legs. They can only walk about on the sea bottom. The largest of the xanthid crabs is the stone crab. It has the biggest claws, too, which it uses to pinch anyone or anything that gets in its way.

Yellow-bellied marmots live in large groups called colonies. When they come out of their rock piles to eat grass, they must be watchful for the hawks and coyotes that eat them. When any member of the colony spots an enemy, it sits up on its hind legs and sounds a shrill warning. Then all the other yellow-bellied marmots pop into their holes.

Zone-tailed hawks can soar for a long time without flapping their wings. When they see a lizard or a mouse on the ground, they go into a steep dive and snatch up the critter with their feet. This high-flying bird builds its nest in a tall tree and decorates it with green leaves.